The
Boy
and
the
Bear

Tracey Corderoy

& Sarah Massini

nosy
Crow

Once upon a time,

there lived a boy

who wanted to play.

But all the best games . . .

like see-saw . . .

and catch . . .

and hide-and-seek
needed two.

And the boy was all alone.

There was Bear, of course.

But Bear was just a bear.

Not a boy who wanted to play.

Besides, Bear was shy.

Too shy even to stop and say hello.

Then, one summer morning,
as the boy sat alone, a paper boat
bobbed across the water.

On the boat was a message.
It said,

"But who would say boo?"
wondered the boy.
"Oh! A Best Friend would
say boo, that's who!"

He quickly wrote back —

— and he sailed his boat across the water.

Then what should come back

but another boat.

Yes!

— wrote the boy —

Wh en?

He waited
    and waited.

Then —

NOW!

— came the reply.
    And out peeped . . .

. . . Bear!

"Oh, it's just you," sighed the boy.
"I thought it might be a Best Friend."

Bear hung his head,
and turned to go.

"Wait!" called the boy. "Come back!
Would you like to play
hide-and-seek?"

With an eager nod, Bear tiptoed
off to hide, and the boy
started to count.

"Ready or not!" he shouted.
"I'm coming!"

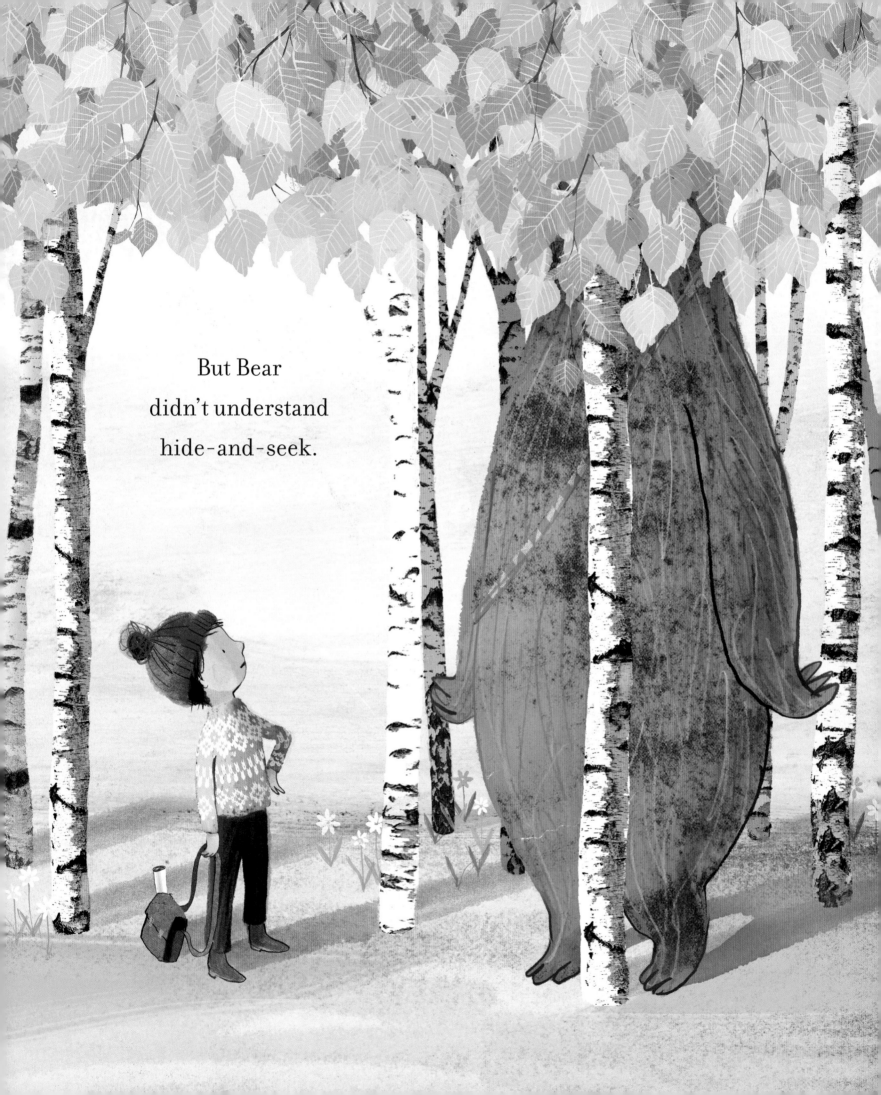

But Bear
didn't understand
hide-and-seek.

And he was too heavy for see-saw.

The next day,

they tried catch.

But that didn't
work either.

Bear couldn't play the boy's games.

"Never mind," sighed the boy.

"We'll just have to think of

something else."

Then, one autumn morning,
Bear **did** think of something.

He started to build . . .

. . . a treehouse!

"Good idea!" said the boy.

"Can I help?"

He passed Bear the logs,

and Bear tied them in place.

Bear knew exactly what to do.

And at last they finished the treehouse, together.

There was a window to gaze out of
at the moon, and a chair
big enough for two.

"Oh, Bear!"
the boy smiled.
"Look what we've made!
It's perfect!"

They stayed in their treehouse
until the leaves
tumbled down . . .

and the first snowflakes fell.

Then, one winter morning,
the boy found a small frosty boat
on the pond.

I MUST GO.

"No!" the boy cried.

"Bear!

Bear!"

But there was no Bear

anywhere.

The boy thought of his friend
through the long chilly days . . .

and the dark starry nights.

He waited all through winter.

But the boy's words froze solid
on the icy pond.

Winter passed and spring came.
Then one morning, as the sun rose,
the boy saw three boats bobbing on the water.

I'M AWAKE!

I MISSED YOU...

ARE YOU THERE?

"Yes! I'm here!"
shouted the boy.
"But where are **you**?"

And out of the trees . . .

came the boy's Best Friend . . .

. . . Bear.